TEENAGE MUTANT *HERO*

TURTLES™

RETURN OF THE TECHNODROME

Written by Mau
Illustrated by (

"HI, GUYS!" It was April O'Neil, TV news-girl from Channel Six. "Anything exciting happening?"

"Actually," said Leonardo, leader of the Teenage Mutant Hero Turtles, "it's been kind of quiet."

"Guess that's why Master Splinter is leaving town," added Donatello, glancing across the underground sewer.

"Is there a story in it?" asked April.

"I'm afraid not," Splinter answered in his deep, humanoid rat voice. "It's merely an annual pilgrimage - three days of fasting and meditation."

"New York's a big city, April," Raphael reminded her. "Something's bound to happen!"

Raphael spoke more truly than he knew. At that very moment, pink-brain Krang was on the Com-Link from Dimension X, glaring savagely at Shredder, sworn enemy of the Turtles!

"You've let those Turtles escape for the last time!" he stormed. "I am bringing the Technodrome back to Earth! Then I shall personally deal with the Turtles!"

"But - Krang…" faltered Shredder, thinking of the gigantic control base, equipped with all its hi-tech electronic wizardry, "you'll need an enormous power source to open a portal that big!"

"Precisely! That's why you, Shredder, are going to take over the Hydro-Electric Station at Niagara Falls!"

Without waiting for any kind of response, Krang snatched up a device to send through the portal to Earth. He watched his monitor to see Shredder had caught it, then issued further instructions.

"Attach this polarity deflector to the main control panel. It will direct the power I need through the portal to the Technodrome!"

Shredder studied the device thoughtfully.

"Well, don't just stand there!" he roared at Rocksteady, his half-human, half-rhino minder. "We must hurry," he raged at Rocksteady's semi-warthog pal, Bebop. "Move!"

Even a half-baked, half-human warthog
and rhino had to be impressed by the
Niagara Falls. Millions of tons of water were
frothing and tumbling, pouring down
hundreds of feet into the Niagara Gorge!

The technicians inside the massive Hydro-
Electricity Station were used to the crash
and the roar of the Falls, so they hardly
noticed one or two extra noises outside.
When the main door was blasted open,
followed by Rocksteady and Bebop bursting
in with their stun-lasers, there was an
instant buzz of fright and confusion.

"What's going on?"

"What's happening?"

But Rocksteady and Bebop were rounding
them up, leaving Shredder to set up the
Com-Link to Dimension X.

"Krang!" Shredder's voice was

triumphant. "I have commandeered the Power Station, and your polarity deflector is in place!"

"For once you've done something right!" growled Krang. "I'll drain the power from this end!"

There was a massive bolt of electrical power, like an enormous flash of lightning, shooting its way from the Hydro-Electric Station towards the river. Here, Krang's portal was already shimmering into solid existence, becoming wider and taller.

As it happened, the Turtles were out of town right then, taking Master Splinter to his secret island retreat. The first they knew about anything being wrong was when the Turtle-Com beeped and April appeared on the mini-screen.

"Fellas, there's been a massive power failure throughout the city! Someone - or something - is draining the power!"

"Krang and Shredder!" exclaimed Leonardo at once. "We'll head back immediately!"

"Yeah!" cried Michaelangelo. "Let's show those creepazoids what Turtle Power is all about!"

Shredder had no idea that the Turtles were on his tail. The Hydro-Electric Station was in his hands, and the turbines screamed as every last atom of power zapped towards the Dimension X portal!

"Yes, it's working!" pink-brain Krang bellowed from the centre of an exo-skeleton body. "Shredder, I'm sending you a contingent of foot soldiers!"

Shredder could hardly believe it! His own foot soldiers! Foot soldiers as good as any the famous Professor Yoshi trained in Japan - before he was forced to flee to America and live in the sewers along with the rats.

That was how he had become 'Master Splinter', when Shredder's radioactive gel flooded the sewer and made him mutant - half-human, half-rat. The same gel mutated his pet turtles, so they became half-turtle, half-teenager.

The loud swish of electric power broke into Shredder's thoughts. A space skimmer carrying the soldiers was being launched from the Technodrome. It zoomed towards the Power Station. There was a pause - then came the sound of marching feet!

"At last!" roared Shredder, as his foot soldiers entered. He snatched up the Com-Link, his voice rising with excitement. "Shredder calling Krang! Come in, Krang!"

"Shredder calling Krang!" There was a lot of crackling on the line, and the Channel Six TV newsroom was plunged into darkness. But Donatello, who was fiddling with the studio's television equipment, knew that voice!

"The soldiers have arrived!"

"Good!" Krang barked on the Turtle-Com screen. *"The Technodrome is almost fully charged! Expect it to come through the portal in approximately..."*

There was another burst of crackling, and Donatello tried frantically to adjust the sound.

"What's he saying?" persisted Raphael.

Donatello hesitated. "I can't make it out... Something about Krang using the Niagara Power Station to open a portal large enough for the Technodrome!

"The Technodrome?" echoed Michaelangelo in disbelief. "Mega disaster!"

"We've got to stop it!" shouted Leonardo,
making a dash for the door. "Turtle
Powwwwerrr!!"

"Wait for me, guys!" yelled April, grabbing
her notebook. "This could be the story of the
century!"

Soon, the Turtles' Blimp airship was
speeding through the sky, with Leonardo
steering the glider section below.

Nobody said too much, each of them
waiting for the first glimpse of Niagara
Falls. Then, above the constant,
breathtaking rush of water, an aggressive
familiar voice floated up towards them.

"Well, well! Look who's here!"

Bebop raised his stun-laser and fired -
slashing the ropes which tethered the glider
to the airship!

"Whoooaaah!" screamed April and the Turtles, as the glider hurtled into the foaming river.

"Safe landing!" panted Leonardo, who was first to recover his breath. "No need to panic!"

"Wanna bet?" cried Donatello, pointing a finger at the foaming crest at the head of the Niagara Falls - the direction in which the glider section was heading! Bebop could not have planned things better if he had tried!

"There's one chance," gasped Donatello, yanking out a remote-control device from his shell. He looked up, checking that the airship was still circling overhead.

"Let's hope Bebop's laser blast didn't damage the remote-control functions..." he murmured, pushing a button and then working a mini joystick.

It seemed like ages before the Blimp turned and began moving down towards the stranded companions!

"It's working!" shouted Leonardo.

"Oh, so tubuloso!" cried Michaelangelo.

Now a hatch was opening in the base of the airship, and a rope unfurled...

"Jump for it!" yelled Leonardo.

They did not need telling twice! Some Turtles grabbed the rope, and the others grabbed the Turtles on the rope. They just made it to safety - a split second before the glider disappeared over the edge of the Falls!

How long they had to hang on by their fingertips, none of them knew. Then, at last, the Blimp drifted down towards a river bank. They had to drop the last few feet, but, how good it felt to be on solid ground again!

"Turtles!" came a familiar friendly voice. "Turtles!"

"Master Splinter!" cried Leonardo. "What are you doing here?"

"That drew me here!" explained Splinter, pointing towards the gigantic portal from Dimension X, as electric power crackled and sparked all around it.

"Krang really is returning the Technodrome to Earth!" gasped Leonardo. "We've got to cut off the power to the portal!"

"The pumps that divert the flow of the river!" shouted Donatello, beginning to sprint up-river. "All we have to do is close them off!"

"Maybe that's why Shredder's got a whole army standing guard by the Pump Station!" observed Raphael drily.

April didn't waste a second - she knew that the sight of a strange girl would confuse the soldiers and distract them from their post.

"Yoo-hoo!" she cried, waving towards the nearest two on patrol! "Hi, fellas!" Then she ran.

The soldiers charged! Where had that girl come from? Where did she go? Surely she must be somewhere around!

"Surprise!" yelled Donatello, leaping in front of the first soldier and hitting out with his Japanese wooden staff, his *bo*. He had forgotten that these particular soldiers were Rock Soldiers from Dimension X who were actually made of rock, so the *bo* simply bounced off!

"Hey!" shouted April again, aiming her Portacam video machine. "You!"

For a moment, Shredder's soldiers stood stock still in amazement - just long enough for Michaelangelo and Donatello to hurl themselves at the Rock Soldiers so that they toppled over the ledge and into the water.

The two Turtles were drenched by two giant splashes!

Meanwhile, Rocksteady was getting bored, being at the Pumping Station all by himself.

"The soldiers should have been back by now," he grumbled to to himself. "What's happened to them?"

"We happened, Rocksteady!" yelled Leonardo, his two swords at the ready.

Right on cue, Raphael sprang up out of the bushes, hurling a knife through the air. It caught the barrel of Rocksteady's stun-laser, jerking it downwards just as it fired!

"What the…?" he began, but Leonardo was already there, leaping with both feet on to Rocksteady's back and knocking him face downwards to the ground.

"Had enough?" he demanded.

Rocksteady was furious with himself, and his anger gave him added strength. He lurched to his feet, flinging Leonardo off balance.

Luckily for the Turtles, Splinter chose that moment to come out of hiding. He flung a handful of orange dust into the humanoid rhino's face!

"Hey!" snorted Rocksteady in fury. "What's…" - he began swaying on his feet, his eyelids drooping "going…   on…   zzzzzzzz…"

Rocksteady crashed to the ground with an almighty thud, snoring as soon as his head hit the turf.

Splinter dusted the last of the powder from his hands, and led the way into the Pump Station.

"We must hurry," he told the Turtles. "The sleep-spice will not affect one of his size for long!"

Leonardo knew they could only have a few minutes before Krang's Technodrome entered through the portal to Earth!

"Okay, Donatello!" he said, racing towards the main control panel. "Shut this thing down!"

"I'll try!" murmured Donatello, flicking a line of switches.

Quite suddenly, there was absolute silence. No sound of water gushing down, no turbines whining at full speed, no loud hum of electricity. The electric power-bolt on which Krang was depending vanished, and the portal began to shrink!

"Krang!" bawled Shredder. "The power has been cut off!"

"I can see that, fool!" Krang snapped back at him. "I'm diverting auxiliary power to the portal!"

There was another series of loud crackles, then the portal began swelling in size, as before. Once again, the Technodrome moved forward, beginning to pass through.

"They must have shut off the pumps!" Shredder roared at Bebop. "Follow me, with

as many soldiers as you can find!"

The Turtles had hardly got outside the
Pumping Station, when a blast from a stun-
laser gun scorched the ground!

"Don't look now, guys," said Raphael,
glancing over his shoulder, "but I think they
figured out our plan!"

At the same time, there was a deep,
rumbling noise, loud enough to make the
ground tremble. For a moment, everyone
stayed quite still, eyes widening.

"Raving ravioli!" breathed Michaelangelo.
"It's the Technodrome!"

And so it was. Every inch of its massive
frame glided through the portal, then
settled on the ground.

"My enemies, the Turtles, are about to be
crushed into amphibian particles!" raved
Krang over the Com-Link. "What a truly
pleasant moment!"

And before the Turtles could turn round,
an enormous hatch had opened. A ramp

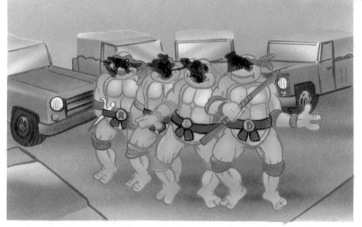

came down and a whole convoy of land
rovers roared into sight, surrounding them
on all sides.

The Turtles could hear Krang's echoing
laugh, even before they saw the
Technodrome's massive laser cannons
swivelling straight towards them.

"I bid you farewell, mutants!"

Krang pressed the switch - but his one
final gale of laughter strangled into snarls
of fury as the lights began flickering. The
glow on the laser cannons fast faded into a
pathetic wisp of light!

"I used too much power in keeping the
portals open!" he raged, frantically working
all the controls he could lay hands on. "The
system is drained!"

Leonardo saw this was their last chance!

"Now, Turtles!" he shouted. "While they're
off guard!"

Brandishing their weapons, they charged forward, leading Splinter and April. They crashed through the ranks of soldiers standing and staring at the Technodrome!

"Stop them!" roared Shredder. "They must not escape!"

Still the Turtles fought on. When one soldier came at Leonardo with a laser gun, the blast rebounded from the blade of a Japanese sword and hit the Technodrome instead! Another beam bounced back, cutting through the largest branch of a tree, knocking a whole crowd of soldiers to the ground!

As for Donatello, he was busy again with his remote control device for the Turtles' Blimp, keeping watch until the airship descended from the sky!

"Keep shooting, you rock-brained morons!" bellowed Bebop, still firing with his laser gun. "They're getting away!"

Somehow the Turtles, Splinter and April managed to sprint towards the rope dangling down from the airship, grabbing it wherever they could. By some miracle, they escaped the laser blasts which scorched the air all around them - but the danger was far from over while the Technodrome was still in Krang's power!

Sure enough, the huge torrents of water were soon falling once again, creating enough electricity to show full power on all the meters inside the Technodrome!

"Splendid!" roared Krang with satisfaction. "Now, to cause the worst earthquake anyone has ever known!"

He turned his exo-skeleton towards Shredder. "I shall take over New York City! From there we shall use the capabilities of Dimension X to conquer the entire planet!"

New York had never seen anything like it. One minute, everyone was going about their normal business, working, shopping, taking children to school...

The next, skyscrapers began swaying like saplings in a hurricane! Cracks split the ground wide open! People began fleeing in panic, tossed around like corks on an ocean!

Still Krang pressed home his attack, using the power of the Hydro-Electric Station to

transmit his pink blob face on every TV set in town!

"This is Krang, Ruler of Dimension X! I command everyone to leave the city immediately! If it is not evacuated in 24 hours, I shall cause a much stronger quake, and level every building to the ground!"

"That's enough!" rapped out Leonardo, leaping to his feet inside the underground sewer lair. "It's time for action!

Leonardo had worked out that, because of its size, Krang's travelling Technodrome must have gouged an enormous, rutted trail beneath the city!

And, with their knowledge of the underground world beneath New York's city streets, it was not too difficult to find where it began...

"If we keep following this trail the Technodrome left," April said, more than once, "we're sure to find it!"

"It's kind of hard to miss!" Raphael agreed, thinking of the massive control centre.

"Look!" Leonardo shouted suddenly, pointing a finger. "There's something up ahead!"

He could hardly have been mistaken. There it was, inside a great cavern which seemed to stretch for miles. The echo of stamping feet proclaimed the presence of teams of soldiers on guard.

"The Technodrome!" breathed Donatello. "We've found it!"

"Getting inside won't be easy," put in Leonardo. "The whole thing is covered with foot-thick Titanium armour!"

"Don't sweat!" advised Donatello, pulling out a high-tech instrument. "I've got this gadget I've been saving for just such an occasion! Everyone take cover!"

The others scrambled towards a line of boulders, only seconds before the device embedded itself in the hull of the Technodrome and exploded with a resounding bang!

Immediately, a light flashed on the Technodrome control panel, and a siren began wailing.

"Security has been breached on Level Seven!" thundered Krang.

"Quickly!" Shredder barked at Rocksteady and Bebop. "Gather a contingent of soldiers and come with me!"

By now, the Turtles, Splinter and April had crawled through the hole made by Donatello's gadget and were looking around at the enormous machinery which powered the Technodrome.

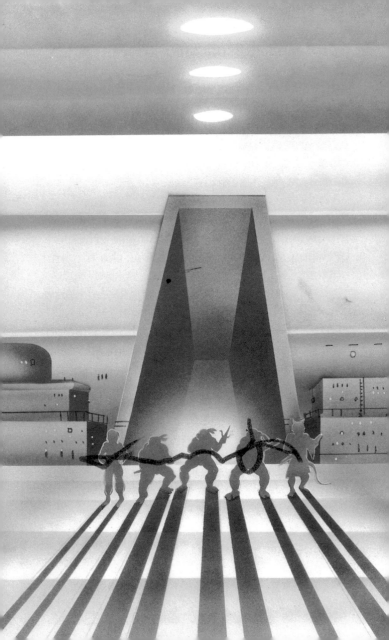

"If I can locate the control circuits," Donatello was saying, wondering where to start, "I can de-activate the earthquake-causing mechanism..."

"Stop!" Splinter held up his hand and his eyes darted around. "Shredder is drawing close. I will lead him away, so that you may continue your search!"

With the sharp eyes of a rat, Splinter found his way to an enormous shaft, where millions of watts of electric power crackled between the giant electrodes at the top and bottom.

Slowly, he began walking along the narrow catwalk which stretched from one side of the shaft to the other. The power bolts flashed on a helmet and visor of steel coming towards him....

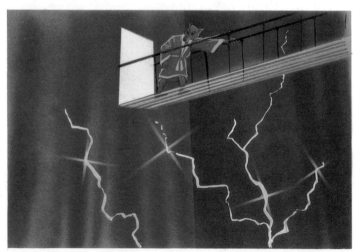

"So, Yoshi," Shredder sounded very pleased with himself. "It is time for our final confrontation!"

"There is no longer a Yoshi," said Splinter, moving forward ready to fight. "Only Splinter!"

"And soon," roared Shredder with his hands raised for combat, "Splinter will be gone as well!"

As for the Turtles, they were still inside the main control room. Donatello was desperately trying to re-wire the circuits!

"Hurry, Donatello!" Leonardo urged him. "We're running out of time!"

"Wrong, turtle-breath!" Bebop cut in. He and Rocksteady stood there, brandishing their stun lasers. "Your time just ran out!"

"You can't fire your lasers in here!" shouted Leonardo, quick as a flash. "You'll damage the Technodrome circuits!"

Bebop and Rocksteady looked at each other, slinging their laser guns over their shoulders. Then, they moved forward, cracking their knuckles ready for another fight!

"Gotcha!" growled Rocksteady, grabbing Leonardo's wrist - which was a mistake. Leonardo simply fell back on to his shell, using his legs to flip Rocksteady over his head and straight into the controls on the wall!

The whole place was plunged into darkness, and there were shouts and crashes, punches and scuffles before the Turtles and April managed to scramble outside.

"Did you have time to shut down the circuits?" April wanted to know.

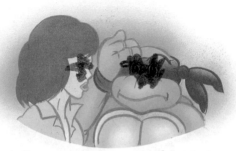

Donatello gave a weary sigh, wiping a flipper across the top of his eye-mask.

"I sure hope so! We'll find out when Krang tries to cause another earthquake!"

His words faltered to a stop as a sinister-sounding rumble reached their ears. Everything looked still and quiet - but further inside the Technodrome, Splinter and Shredder were still fighting, each determined to beat the other.

Then, the whole shaft had begun to shake so hard that the catwalk swayed violently. Both Shredder and Splinter struggled to hold on. Next minute, a power bolt came lancing down, slicing through the catwalk!

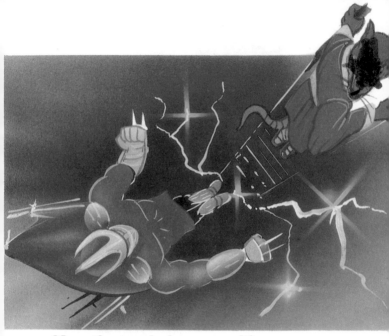

Now, the two halves were like a rope
bridge cut in two, with Splinter and
Shredder clinging desperately to each
section, a bottomless pit beneath them!

Splinter could see his only chance was to
use the sagging catwalk railing like a
ladder, and he climbed up to safety.

Shredder was not so lucky. His cape had
caught on a jagged edge - so he could only
dangle there, shaking an armoured fist!
"Curse you, Splinter!" he cried.

April and the Turtles had already escaped
through the hole which Donatello had blown
in the hull of the Technodrome. Then a

familiar brown, furry figure came leaping out of the hole to join them.

"Let's haul shell!" shouted Donatello, leading the way out. "That thing's about to drill straight down to the earth's core!"

Donatello was not exaggerating. Krang, on the bridge of the Technodrome could feel the whole thing fast descending below the level of the cavern floor!

"Someone has reversed the seismic polarities!" he stormed. "The Technodrome is sinking!"

A mass of molten lava began bubbling up as the Technodrome bit deeper into the earth. Then fumes rose from the earth's core, swirling around the Technodrome like a thick cloud!

"Shredder!" thundered Krang, his voice getting fainter and fainter with every centimetre the Technodrome sank into the boiling lava. "This is all your fault! I'll get you for thi-i-i-s..."

There were a few more plops and gurgles. Then, all was quiet.

The moment everything was back to normal, April, the Turtles and Splinter decided to throw a pizza party to celebrate!

"What a story!" April kept saying. "Krang and Shredder, defeated by four half-teenagers and half-turtles!"

"Hey," Raphael butted in, "let's not forget one half-man and half-rat!"

A slow smile spread across April's pretty face. "Know something, guys?" she said, looking around the sewer, "I just realised, I'm the only one hundred per cent human being in this place!"

"Aw, don't feel bad, April!" grinned Michaelangelo. "Nobody's perfect!"